CYBERHACKER

BY ANSON MONTGOMERY

ILLUSTRATED BY ERIC CHERRY

An R. A. Montgomery Book

BANTAM BOOKS
NEW YORK • TORONTO • LONDON • SYDNEY • AUCKLAND

RL 4, ages 8–12

CYBERHACKER

A Bantam Book / May 1998

CHOOSE YOUR OWN ADVENTURE® is a registered trademark of Bantam Books, a division of Bantam Doubleday Dell Publishing Group, Inc.
Registered in U.S. Patent and Trademark Office and elsewhere.

Original conception of Edward Packard

Cover art by Romas Kukalis
Interior illustrations by Eric Cherry

ISBN 0-553-56747-0

Published simultaneously in the United States and Canada

Bantam Books are published by Bantam Books, a division of Bantam Doubleday Dell Publishing Group, Inc. Its trademark, consisting of the words "Bantam Books" and the portrayal of a rooster, is Registered in U.S. Patent and Trademark Office and in other countries. Marca Registrada. Bantam Books, 1540 Broadway, New York, New York 10036.

PRINTED IN THE UNITED STATES OF AMERICA

CWO 0 9 8 7 6 5 4 3 2 1

To my family, my friends, and, of course, to Rebecca

WARNING!

This book is not like other books you have read. In this story, *you* choose what happens next. There are many different endings, so you can read this book over and over again, and it will be different every time.

As you read, you'll have the chance to decide what will happen. Whenever you make a decision, turn to the page shown. What happens to you next in the story depends on your choices.

You're a computer hacker in the year 2098. The virtual reality dives you make inside the computer—or Cyberverse—are risky. Sometimes people never return from the 'verse. But when your best friend disappears, you have to help find him. Should you go in on your own or call the police for help? Choose carefully—there's danger at every turn!

It's your choice. Your thrills. *Your* adventure!

You float through the haze, trying to track the tiny glowing particles that swim back and forth like minnows in a pool. Each particle delivers its charge to your energy matrix. After a tiring but enjoyable chase, your job is complete. As you make your way to the nearest interface gateway, you wonder how this part of the mainframe became contaminated. It's probably just some random feedback, you think.

But now is not the time for thinking. Reintegration is always difficult. Calming yourself, you focus on transferring your consciousness back into your physical body.

"Are you back?" a voice asks you.

Unable to speak at first, you simply nod.

"Did you track down the interference?"

"Yup. But that's not all," you say with a smile. "I went ahead and cleared out the random charges that were interfering with the microprocessor. There were just too many charges. They must have been building up for a long time, so that rules out sabotage."

"Well, just so long as the computer is working now," Principal Donner says with obvious relief.

"Can I go back to class now?" you ask.

"Of course. And thank you for your help. I'm not sure what we would have done without you."

"Just remember that when you send home my grades!" you reply.

⟶

2

As a self-taught disk rider in the virtual world called the Cyberverse, you have become your high school's cheap and convenient answer to a computer repair person—and you're only in ninth grade! But you don't mind. Any chance to experience the freedom of the virtual world excites you. Reality in the twenty-first century is just too slow and boring. You prefer the Cyberverse—or, as you call it, the 'verse.

There's another reason why you're a disk rider. The world of 2098 is a tough one. Your father's been out of work for a while, and your family can really use the extra credits you make.

You stroll back to class and slide into the seat behind your computer screen. Mrs. Hargrove, the instructor, is going over computer programming material you learned when you were eight. You put your head down, hoping to take a quiet nap, but just as you are about to drift off . . .

"So what did they have you do?" your friend Greg whispers in your ear. You look up at him and see that he has his computer illegally hooked into the Battle Arena. The arena is a sort of game in which players fight each other for Cyberverse supremacy and money. Students are universally banned from such areas of the Cyberverse.

→

"Just the usual. A full-body immersion to track down some charged particle fields that were interfering with the mainframe's functions. I have no idea how those particles were attracted to that specific site," you reply.

"Just another mystery of the technological world that we inhabit," Greg replies.

"I guess so. Now let me sleep," you say. You know that you will be cut some slack since you've helped the principal out.

"Hey," Greg says after a few more minutes.

"What?" you groan sleepily.

"I heard there's a place somewhere in the industrial sector of the 'verse where you can get access to codes that were banned after the Information Protocols were instituted."

"Really?" you say, suddenly alert. You have never explored the industrial sector. It's highly monitored. You've heard rumors that some companies keep illegal software there. No one knows what this software does, but it is definitely something that goes against the Global Law Information Protocols that were instituted in 2047.

"Well, I'm sure that your conversation is *extremely* interesting, but I do have a class to teach." Mrs. Hargrove is staring at you and Greg. "While this material might be simple for you two, I have others in the class who are eager to learn."

→

4

You're not so sure the rest of the class wants to learn, but you know that sometimes silence is the best policy. Greg follows your lead and even tries to look ashamed. Mrs. Hargrove can't really give you a bad grade in the course, considering that you had to help her with some of the material, but you don't want to get a "bad attitude" mark in your report.

As she goes back to lecturing the class at the holoboard, a message pops up on your computer screen. "MEET ME AT 6:00 IN THE PUBLIC ACCESS TERMINAL BANKS ON THE 12TH LEVEL.—G." You nod at Greg.

The rest of the day crawls by. During gym class you are the first one thrown into the Black Hole in Gravity Ball. A forty-five-minute wait floating on your back in complete darkness is just what you need after the job you did for Principal Donner. Finally the school day ends, and you head to the public access terminals to meet Greg.

You hurry down the corridor among a rushing crowd of businesspeople, merchants, students, and tourists, keeping your eyes open for Greg. Then you see him. His royal blue unisuit flashes erratically, and you figure that his power supply must be malfunctioning.

"What took you so long?" he barks.

"Sorry. Things just did not flow today," you answer.

"Well, do you have the power booster?"

"Of course I do," you reply, as you enter one of the empty public access booths. Greg squeezes in behind you as the door automatically begins to close. You pull the booster out of your backpack. Greg constructed the booster to allow both of you to do full body immersions from the public terminal. This way, all your senses can be transported into the Cyberverse, and you can interact with other people or programs instead of merely getting information. With the booster, you can do everything you can from your more powerful home units but without monitoring from your parents . . . or anyone else. It's difficult to track down a Cyberverse user who's at a public access terminal.

With two practiced twists, you attach the booster. Now you can float free in the Cyberverse. Maybe you'll be able to find the codes Greg was talking about and make some extra credits.

6

INSERT 4.8 CREDITS FOR THE FIRST HALF HOUR OF USE, the console informs you. Greg pantomimes pulling out empty pockets, and you reluctantly slide your debit card into the slot. Hopefully this expedition will take less than a half hour.

"Ready?" Greg asks.

"Yup. Let's do it."

As you place the helmets over your heads, you prepare yourself for the reality shift about to take place. You are about to experience a computer-generated simulation of reality. Full immersion into the Cyberverse involves many risks. Each "dive" presents real dangers. You've heard of disk riders whose brains became permanently convinced that the Cyberverse was reality. Such people become trapped forever in the 'verse.

Turn to page 12.

INSERT 4.0 CREDITS FOR FIRST HALF HOUR OF USE

8

Insects the size of large dogs fly haphazardly about and dark clouds skitter across the sky. Scattered trees dip their branches into the gray water, where rippling shapes twist and fight for position and food.

"Now what?" you ask.

"I'm not sure," Heran replies, "but I don't think we should stand around here. I've heard rumors about monsters that track down players."

"Let's head toward someplace drier. I don't think we want to go into that water," you say. You move away from the dark shapes writhing under the murky water and toward the denser forest.

As soon as you get onto firmer ground, your vision is restricted by the trees and numerous vines drooping off the branches like greasy hair.

Tramping through the dark swamp, you are overwhelmed by the unfairness of your situation. You stop paying close attention to your surroundings.

Without warning four figures drop out of the trees above you. They slide down the vines before you can react. Two come at you, and two at Heran. "Watch out!" you call to Heran, even as your own legs are captured in a tight grip. Looking up, you see a humanoid figure with green skin and a wide mouth. A flippered hand strikes out, and you crumple to the ground. The last thing you see is a froglike creature leaping into the air. Then everything goes black.

Turn to page 40.

You decide to help by searching the databases, something you are good at. One quick scan and you'll be able to tell if Greg's or the other missing persons' mental signatures are in a particular database. The only problem is that you need complete access to each computer's central processing unit. For this you'll have to actually enter the computers in the Cyberverse.

"Okay, you are in charge of sectors D45 through G17," the officer in charge tells you. "Give each one a careful look, but don't waste any time. We have a lot of searching to do, and it's easy to get sidetracked."

You try to remember his words as you go through computer after computer, but sometimes confusions cannot be avoided. Each computer is set up differently, and the multitude of strange environments distracts you from the job at hand. The search goes on for days, and you settle into a routine.

You wake up, go to the police station, send confirmation to your school that you are still on police business, and then search until late at night. Frustration and exhaustion make you want to quit, but you must help your friend. No matter what.

Three days into the search, the words "We've found them" come over the communications line. You start to cry with relief. "They seem to be all right, just a bit confused and weak." Even though you did not make the actual discovery, it's good to know that you helped.

The End

10

Greg's parents are in his room waiting for you when you return to the physical world. The worried looks on their faces change quickly to flashes of anger. You decide that it would be a good idea to get out of there fast. You rush home to your own worried parents.

Your mom and dad have lots to say to you. Basically, they forbid you to enter the Cyberverse again. They have even altered their own on-line account so that you are now excluded from the 'verse, except for homework access.

The only problem is, in all this excitement, you get a sudden flash about where Shenda might have been taken. But to make sure, you will need to do a full immersion. When Shenda mentioned she had some cyberrands, or errands to do in the virtual world, you thought she meant ordinary stuff. Now you suspect that she was going in to check on something else. The officer who interrogated you let slip that Shenda was trying to get information on a group stealing food credits from the poor. Maybe someone didn't like the fact that she was looking for this information.

$\longrightarrow$

Each moment that Shenda remains missing, the less chance you have of finding her healthy and safe. If you do go back into the Cyberverse, you'll have to take precautions. This time you'll let the police know what you are doing, but only *after* you have started. A simple notifying program will take care of that.

But why should you risk your life again? Maybe nothing bad has happened to her at all. Maybe you should just tell the police what you know and leave it at that.

If you decide to defy your parents' orders and search for Shenda in the Cyberverse, turn to page 56.

If you choose to let the police handle the search while you tell them what you know, turn to page 73.

12

Suddenly everything goes blue. You are suspended in a semiliquid environment. Bits of data float by like fish. You see big round objects with spikes protruding—the well-protected computer hard drives of various individuals and small businesses. Turning left, you see Greg. With a simple glance and a wave of your arm, you move forward in the direction of the nexus, where all of the various computers attached to the Cyberverse meet. From the nexus you can catch data currents to almost any section of the 'verse.

"Let's head for the industrial sector," you tell Greg through the communications unit in your helmet. Back in the physical world, your helmet and Greg's are connected directly by a cable, which prevents anyone from listening to your conversation.

Turn to page 68.

All twenty members of the tracking team, including you, have special virtual bodies made for speed, communication, and defense. As a probe unit, the officers can use their abilities to discover the whereabouts of particular individuals and then apprehend them.

"Nelson!" the commander barks. "You're in charge of the kid. Stay in control, and don't be afraid to bug out with the civilian. The last thing we want are upset parents."

"Yes, sir!"

"Now, we are going to go back to the data-trail that we froze on the original rescue mission. We're looking for links, but remember that our suspect is a real pro, and they all have to be well hidden. Make sure, don't guess."

You stay silent throughout the briefing. The team files into a program that will transport you back to the games access level, which, unlike everything else, was not destroyed in the self-destruct sequence.

"Stay close to me, kid," Nelson tells you, "and if you see the suspect, let me know." You copy his actions as he links up to the transport program.

Turn to page 62.

Grabbing hold of the hook at the end of the cable, you flick a switch on the winch unit. You hope it will let you down slowly. You hang on tightly as the hook drops through the air. During your trip down, a giant eagle flies close and screams at you but leaves without attacking.

When you get to the ground, the winch keeps working, and the metal line bunches up in a haphazard coil. Suddenly you feel a tap on your shoulder. Reacting instinctively, you reach up and grab a strange hand. Then you lean forward and flip the owner of the hand onto the still-descending line.

"Owwww!" the person yells.

"Who are you?" you ask, as you move forward and put your knee on the person's neck.

"Lemme go!" shouts a girl about your age. "I'm not an enemy. I'm a player like you!"

"What do you mean?" You don't take your knee away.

"Are you new?" your captive asks. This time there is wonder in her voice. "Has someone else been added? Why are you here? Do you know how to get out?"

"Yes, I am new, and I have no idea what is going on here," you say. "Can you tell me?"

"Well, first of all, you can let me up. I'm not going to attack you. And then we should get out of here. The gorillas usually make a full round every ten minutes."

Turn to page 85.

You decide to try entering the access hatch into the brown building. Following the probes will just increase your chances of being observed. You don't know what entering the hatch will entail, but you hope for the best.

"It's now or never," you mutter, wishing Greg were with you.

The hatch is opened by a simple lever. It seems odd to you that there is no lock, but you shrug your shoulders and lift it up.

The entrance leads to a dimly lit tunnel. As you move along it, you wonder why the designers made the plan so similar to an actual access tunnel in the physical world. Just lack of imagination, you think.

You have been traveling along the tunnel for a while when suddenly a black barrier appears in front of you. You turn around and see the same type of barrier behind. You are trapped!

"INSERT IDENTIFICATION CARD NOW. YOU HAVE FIVE SECONDS," commands a computerized voice.

$\longrightarrow$

Searching your virtual body frantically, you realize that you don't have *anything* to put in the slot, let alone an identification card. There is nothing that you can do, so you wait. The wait is not long. As soon as the five seconds are up, you find yourself sliding down a tube that has opened in the floor beneath you.

The ride down the tube is short. You land in a red foam haze like the one that attacked you and Greg the other day. You are unable to move—and this time you cannot reach your recall button. Your hope that you will be recalled into the physical world when your time runs out at the terminal fades as you remain stuck long past your paid time.

Turn to page 66.

"Great match, folks! To show our appreciation, we are going to bestow an honor on the winner." Thunder explodes with each word this being speaks. The green player just stands there, his six arms folded and his shield on his back.

"You have fought a valiant battle," continues the announcer, "and as a reward, you will receive an automatic program erasure bundle. Any opponent or obstacle that you encounter in the swamp will be instantly removed. You may use it only once."

As you listen to the voice booming above you, you get an idea. It is risky. If you could get to the erasure bundle, which is floating in front of the tower, you might be able to change the rules of the game. The problem is, you don't know if the bundle will work for you or how you are going to get it. You have only a few moments to make up your mind.

If you decide to try to steal the erasure bundle, turn to page 33.

If you want to challenge the green player for an even better prize, turn to page 36.

"Not a full one," Officer Nelson replies from behind you. "We lost the equipment for a multiuser tracker and transporter. All we have left is the one-person tracer-link that I have in my commander's kit. Only one of us can follow the old man, and we also need some-one to take the hostages back to safety while the squad wraps up these monsters."

If you decide to go after the old man by using the link, turn to page 58.

If you choose to stay and help the hostages, turn to page 48.

"Whoever created this little world must be insane," Police Sergeant Drusta says. His breath smells of processed synthomeat. "Selling such a complex system to any of the entertainment conglomerates would instantly make the inventor wealthy beyond imagination."

"I doubt he was doing it for money," you say, remembering how the old man said his work wasn't appreciated. "He seemed to be doing it for art's sake."

"Sarge," a uniformed officer interrupts. "We just got word in from the tracking team. Four of the missings have been traced to the area where we rescued this one." He glances at you. "I'm afraid that one of them is your friend Greg. He disappeared after alerting us to your situation."

"Hmm," Drusta says, wiping his hands on his uniform. "I imagine that the old guy will try to get rid of those witnesses as soon as possible. We'll need to do another wide sweep and get a team after the guy. Round up everyone we can get."

→

"I'll help," you say, trying to forget how tired you are. The last thing you want to do is to put your life back in the hands of the old man, but Greg needs you. And Heran is still stuck in the game, too.

"Good," Drusta says without turning away from the other officer. "We can use you. You can either go with the tracking team and help them identify the perpetrator, or you can help with the database search."

If you decide to go with the tracking team, turn to page 29.

If you choose to search for Greg and the others through the databases, turn to page 9.

"They should be fine, but we need to repair any serious damage to their virtual bodies before sending them back to the physical world. Too much damage on this side can result in massive shock during reintegration."

"Oh," you say. "Can I see my friends Heran and Greg?"

The doctor stops for a moment. "You're not supposed to, but I'll let you see Greg. Heran is fine but still unconscious. Greg will be all right, too. I just left him. He was starting to regain consciousness in his virtual body." The doctor leads the way to Greg's room.

"Does it hurt?" you ask Greg as you stand over the bed in which he is resting.

"Find the pyramid," he says.

"How do you feel?"

"The pyramid," he says, sitting up. You realize that he is trying to tell you something important.

"What about the pyramid?" you ask. But Greg lapses back into unconsciousness before he can answer.

Taking a gamble, you call Lieutenant O'Reilly on your com-link and tell him that the pyramid might be important.

"Thanks kid, but I'm kind of busy," he replies.

Turn to page 103.

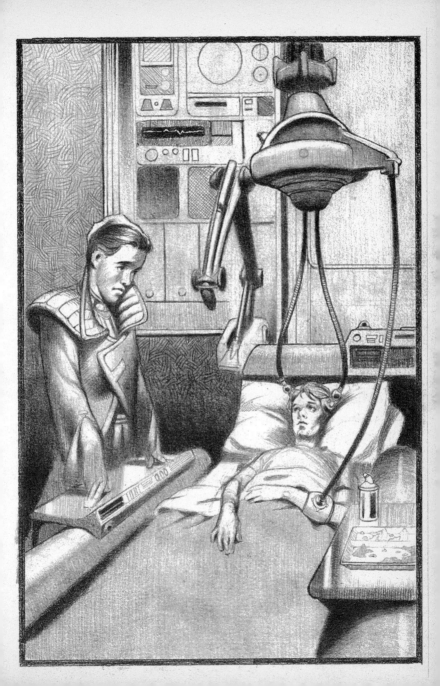

Once you are out of the Food Wheel, Shenda hurries you along the corridors to a private vehicle access port. With a quick shove she sends you stumbling into the front seat of a luxury float-car. She gets in behind you, but your attention is focused on the neatly dressed man sitting in one corner of the backseat. He does not greet you, but you know two things: You are not with the police, and this man is in charge.

"You are a foolish young person, meddling in matters that are beyond your comprehension," he tells you. "But at least you are not a police informer. That is the only mark in your favor. You obtained more information than you thought when you attempted to violate our data banks. One of my subordinates has retrieved that data from your house. Luckily for you, all of it was there and undisturbed."

"What do you want with me?" you ask.

"Nothing really. Just to warn you never to interfere with one of our operations again. The only reason that you are alive now is your refusal to cooperate with the police. Do not tell anyone of this meeting. Now get out of my car."

With that, the door opens and you climb out, still confused, but alive. As the float-car flies away, Shenda leans out one of the windows and waves to you.

"See you later, kid!" she yells.

The End

Maybe you can shove the old man and his pet beast out the hole. As if sensing your thoughts, the beast growls from its corner. The old man stares at you intently.

If you try to fix the alert tag at the table, turn to page 55.

If you decide to grab the tag and jump back down to the game, turn to page 52.

26

When you come to again, you are in the public terminal, sprawled on the floor. Greg lies next to you, still unconscious. As you shake him, you see that the booster is now just a blackened piece of melted junk. The thought that this might just as easily have happened to your head makes your stomach turn.

"What happened?" Greg asks when you finally manage to wake him.

"I'm not sure," you answer. "But those people definitely do not want their information disturbed."

"Well, I for one am willing to let them have it." Greg shakes his head. "Wow, that was *not* fun. If I hadn't managed to hit the disconnect, we might still be in there."

You don't like to think about such things. You and Greg say good-bye, and you stagger to the magnatrain. Once home, you tiptoe past your mom, who's sleeping on the couch in the living room. You just want to relax and wind down. As you lie on your bed, you notice that the mail light on your computer screen is blinking. You open the message and read it on the screen.

Turn to page 93.

"Neither option sounds too promising," you say.

"No. But after being here for over a year, I'm so desperate that I'll try anything. If you help, maybe we can make it together."

"You don't know anything about who set this whole thing up?"

"Nope," Heran replies. "All I know is that I was hacking into this database—and then *blammo*, I'm stuck in here with a bunch of gorillas chasing me. After that, I found my secure spot two levels away. The gorillas don't bother me there, and I can rest." She glances around nervously. "We really should get out of here before they return."

If you decide to go with Heran through the challenge rounds, turn to page 98.

If you want to try getting through the swamp, turn to page 49.

28

Hoping your camouflage will continue to work, you follow the probes. Eventually they stop before one of the doors. It opens. The probes dump your duplicate inside the room.

With a start, you move backward as the probes turn around and head straight for you. At first you think they might have observed your presence, but then you realize they are just returning to guard duty. You move into another corridor and wait for them to pass before returning to the door that your duplicate was tossed through.

The number on the door is thirty-nine. You try to think. Shenda should logically be in room thirty-seven, since your last duplicate was no doubt placed in room thirty-eight. You knock on the door to room thirty-seven but get no response. You are considering forcing the door open when you hear movement down the corridor and see figures coming toward you. You have to get out of here.

The return trip through the network is as fast as before but seems to take an eternity. By the time you get back, your hour and a half is about up. You hit your recall button.

Turn to page 53.

29

You decide to go with the tracking team. The commanding officer, Lieutenant O'Reilly, gathers you and the other members of the team together. "We're going to do this by the numbers, people," he says. "I want everyone to focus on what is happening, not on personal glory. If our information is correct, the suspect has been responsible for kidnapping citizens and placing them in a virtual death-world. Since we are going after him, we have to play by his rules. Keep a sharp lookout for traps, and don't get dead."

Turn to page 13.

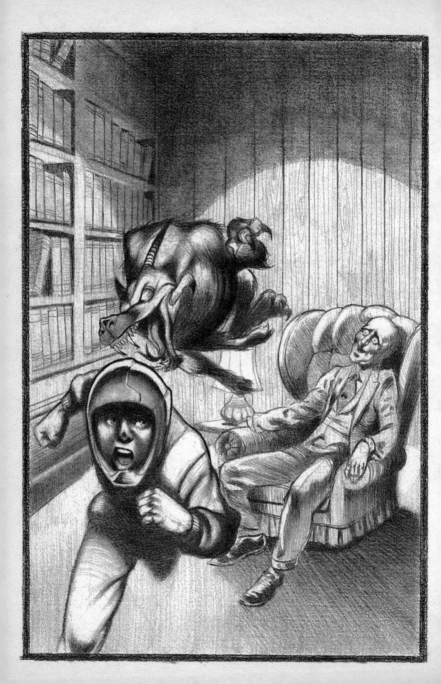

"My name does not matter," the old man replies. "And now the game shall start anew. Do not try using your crude tag programs. They have all been rendered inoperative. Besides, Gorgo would rip you to shreds before your hand reached the table."

You don't know what else to do, so you run for the door. In one sure leap, Gorgo lands on your back and bites into your neck. You fall to the carpeted floor once again and lie still.

The old man laughs. "You are amusing, so I'm going to give you a reward. The program will take just a moment, but it will last a long time. We can always use another gorilla to help guard the entrance level, and you'll be perfect for the job. You will enjoy eternity as a gorilla chasing down any other thieves who try to steal my secrets."

The End

You pull at the bars of your cage, causing your prison to swing wildly back and forth. The bars seem too strong to break with your fists, but if you could crash the cage against something else, they might give way. Looking to your left, you see that Heran's cage could hit yours if you got both swinging. Then you would just have to avoid the hungry water residents. You try not to think about that yet.

You have to get out of here one way or the other, and you have to do it soon. If the frog-beings come back, you have the feeling your game will be over—permanently. Should you break the cages or have Heran activate her prize?

If you ask Heran to activate her prize, turn to page 60.

If you break open the cages by smashing them against each other, turn to page 51.

You make up your mind to try to get the erasure bundle. Quickly you begin moving toward the tower. "Cover me!" you yell back to Heran. You hope she can do something to protect you. No one has noticed you yet. You get ready to leap for the erasure bundle.

"Stop!" the voice from above yells, but you pay no attention. You are watching the player still in his battle body, and you realize that he sees you. A fist the size of your body comes down at you. With a burst of speed you avoid it, but the force of the blow on the sand behind you makes you stumble. Waiting for the next fist to finish you off, you see a flash of movement in the farthest corner of your vision.

"Go now!" you hear Heran scream as she runs straight at the green player. In the moment that he is distracted, you manage to continue running. You jump as high as you can and grab the erasure bundle. *One down,* you think, as you fall face forward onto the sand.

Turn to page 44.

"Thought that you were going to be the hero? I like that—it makes my task that much more enjoyable."

"Do whatever you want," you manage to say. "The police will continue to search, and they will find you."

"I'll chance it. But right now, I think I am going to get out of here and initiate the self-destruct sequence. I always make a grand exit."

You wait, knowing that your time in this virtual world will soon be up.

The End

Before you left your house, you wrote up a very simple program that copies the three-dimensional image of your virtual body. Using such a copy, you can make it appear as though someone is trying to break into the data bank without having to risk getting your virtual body caught in a trap. With a quick command, you generate the body-copy and send it toward the building. You move back and hide yourself behind another structure.

As you watch, a shimmering screen seems to envelop the copy of your virtual body, which then disappears. Before it vanishes, you catch a glimpse of what look like four separate tracking probes attaching themselves to the copy.

You get an idea. Hitting the copy button again, you send another body at the data bank. But this time you're going to follow it. The body-copy will be a decoy. You'll follow it with a camouflage program running to hide your presence.

A shimmer of light surrounds the copy as it nears the building, but this time the four tracking probes do not immediately appear. You activate the camouflage program and pass through the shimmering screen yourself.

Turn to page 84.

36

"I'm going to challenge the green player," you tell Heran.

"Okay," Heran says, but her voice sounds doubtful.

Before you know it, your virtual body has been over-lapped with that of a huge, blue, human-faced scor-pion. You have long, shell-covered arms ending in pincers. Each pincer holds a curved sword. You swing them loosely to practice. Above your head bobs the point of your tail. A wicked stinger glistens with poi-son. You realize that you understand exactly how to strike with its deadly tip.

Across from you is a mirror image of your present body. The other scorpion is an identical replica of you, except for the color of its scales, which are bright pink.

"Begin," the announcer's voice intones. The crowd hushes.

With two swift moves, your opponent is on top of you. A combination of sword and tail strikes forces you to drop your right sword. You feel a burning pain in your right pincer and see the mark of your opponent's stinger. You swing feebly with your left hand, but your sword bounces off the tough armor of your opponent. Turning and running, you almost make it to your rest area.

Almost.

The End

38

There is no telling what that red spot really is. You climb down the tree as quickly as you can. Just as you make it to the base, you hear a grunt from the other side, followed by the noise of tearing bark. You freeze. All you can do is hope the gorillas pass by you. You wonder if animals in the Cyberverse have a sense of smell.

As the sound of the gorillas fades away above you, you scramble down into the system of roots and swing out. There is no ground. The tree grows out of midair. Holding on to two long-trailing roots, you swing your body to get as much momentum as possible. Launching into the air takes all the courage you possess.

Twisting as you fall, you travel headfirst into the uppermost branches of a weeping willow. The wood gives way, and you are stunned by the impact. Eventually you manage to drag your virtual body out of the tree's canopy and to the main trunk. No other trees are visible from the top of this willow, so you decide to check out the situation at its roots.

As you climb down the tree you notice something unusual. What looks like a winch is attached to one of the tree's spreading branches. It has a long coil of cable strung around its drum and a large hook at the bottom so big you think you could stand on it. It may not be a traditional elevator, but right now you need any help you can get.

Turn to page 15.

You stare at her in surprise for a moment. "How do you know about me, and why are you so interested in what I do?" you finally ask.

She takes a moment or two before replying.

"First of all, my name is Shenda, and I saw what happened to the two of you by accident. I was exploring on my own, and the 'brown building' mainframe was the focus of my expedition. Rumors around the 'verse led me to it as a possible source of renegade code. That's when I saw you and your buddy."

"Then why didn't you help us when we were caught in the foam?"

"Why didn't I get myself as stuck as you—someone I don't even know—for no reason? You tell me."

"I'm sorry," you say quickly, "but your mysterious message and this little meeting hasn't really helped my peace of mind."

"Well, we need your help, and you need ours. If you keep on exploring the way you have been, you're going to end up caught in some twentieth-century PC in the middle of nowhere," Shenda says.

"What do you mean 'we'?"

"The Cyberverse Police Force. I am a fully authorized deputy—when I'm not in school, that is."

You sit there, horrified. All you can think is that any second the rest of the CPF is going to show up and arrest you for infocrimes. Shenda goes on quietly eating her lunch.

Turn to page 88.

40

Gradually you regain consciousness. For a brief moment you expect to wake in your physical body in your room at home. But the reality of your situation shatters that notion. You are still in the virtual swamp, trapped in a wicker cage above the swirling waters. Your entire body—virtual or not—is pulsing with deep pain. Tentacles reach out of the water toward your cage.

"Are you all right?" you hear from a short distance away. You turn to see Heran in a cage to your left. She is covered in mud.

"I'll be fine," you say. "But how are we going to get out of here?"

"I have one prize," Heran replies. You can hear fear in her voice. "I found it at the base of one of the trees back in the gorilla zone. It might help us. But there are booby traps all over the place. Most of the easily found prizes either do nothing or something useless. And some hurt whoever uses them."

"Hold on," you mumble as you see the frog-beings gathering under the trees near your cages. One by one they step onto something and then disappear. It must be a transport platform. If you could get to it, you could get out of this place.

Turn to page 32.

"Where am I?" you ask when you come to and see the rows of desks and rushing people.

"The Cyberverse police station," Heran replies. You notice that she sounds more in control than before. "You have just been processed through module Seven-Gamma, Individualistic Reconditioning. The game scenario was created to help troubled youths become healthy members of the Cyberverse. You needed to learn compassion, teamwork, and self-sacrifice. I was the case officer assigned to the procedure, and you passed with great style."

You are stunned. "What—What do you mean? Who are you?"

"You were assigned this reconditioning based on your problems with infotrusion," she says without pausing. "I am Deputy Shenda. I am sorry that I had to deceive you, but the program was a success."

You do not know what to say, and you are not sure if you completely agree with her conclusions. But you do know that you won't be doing any more unauthorized hacking.

The End

You decide to jump into the red spot. You leap up and throw your body at the shimmering space. You hit your target perfectly and land with a thump on your stomach. You're lying on the floor of a carpeted room.

Before you looms a strange creature with uneven horns and a snout that sharpens to a point. Its black tongue pokes between its teeth. Huge shoulders bunch up behind its head. You lie still on the floor.

"Thought you were getting out easy, did you?"

You jump at the voice. You think it was the creature in front of you that spoke, but its mouth did not move.

"I was talking to you," the voice continues. "Do not ignore me, for I am in control here."

You see that the owner of the voice is a gnarled old man, and not the beast, which appears to be some sort of pet. The man wears a neat pinstriped suit.

"Excuse me," you say with a start. "I was just trying to get away from those gorillas."

"Just because you made it to the study room does not mean that you are out of trouble," the old man says. "Did you like the gorillas? It is so hard to get all the details right."

The beast slouches over to a rug in front of a fireplace. You sit up and glance around the room. Off to one side is a table cluttered with tools used to create computer programs. This man must be the creator of the game you were just trapped inside.

Turn to page 83.

Soon, however, you are lost. Nothing in the landscape is distinct enough to act as a landmark. You begin to get the feeling that you are traveling in circles.

"This is useless," you finally say, after hours of trudging along inside the sphere. "How do we make it out of this place?"

"I don't know," Heran replies in a small voice. "Maybe this is just a big trick, and there *is* no way out."

"Of course there is," you say. "We just have to keep searching."

Turn to page 92.

44

Raising your head, you see the tower right in front of you. The sky has darkened. A vertical line appears and shatters the sky into infinite fragments. A black hole now floats there, and white gorillas, giant flying insects, and countless other creatures start to pour out from it. A laser blast hits the ground next to you. The sand turns to glass.

Grabbing the bundle, you get up, leap for the tower, and begin climbing.

A creature—half man and half frog—springs up ahead of you onto the tower. You grab its flippered foot and drag it off before it can get its balance. You trigger the erasure bundle by hitting the big button on its side.

Turn to page 69.

46

A great pyramid houses the Well. Banners and tenting surround the whole structure. Humanoid shapes fill all the spaces you can see. Many can consult with the Well at once, but many more wait patiently for their chance. You and Greg get in line.

When it's your turn, you step up to the Well and ask your question: "I want to know whether the person known as Shenda is an official member of the Cyberverse Police Force, and if so, what her duties are?"

"Please enter data first," a disembodied voice replies.

"Okay . . . I'm not sure if this is the sort of stuff that you want, but—my younger brother, Tom, is afraid of horses."

"Accepted. The young woman known as Shenda is affiliated with the Cyberverse Police Force, but she is not a full officer of the law. She has been assigned to special operations within the Cyberverse."

"Thank you," you say, and begin to leave. But as you move toward the exit you notice the blazing blue uniforms of the Cyberverse police. Then you see Greg being held firmly in the center of six officers. All the officers have their battle program software activated and at the ready.

→

"You are being arrested for the abduction and kidnapping of Special Deputy Shenda Lang. Please come with us," one of the officers says in a deep voice.

You wonder what to do. With your modified safety recall button, you can be back in Greg's room before they know it. Once there, you can get in touch with a lawyer or simply collect your thoughts and try to figure out what is going on. On the other hand, you don't want to abandon Greg.

If you decide to try to make a break for it, turn to page 72.

If you try to explain what has happened to the police, turn to page 75.

48

"You go after him," you yell to Officer Nelson. "I'll take care of the hostages. That way you won't have to look out for me."

"Right," he says. "Take this expansion net and bring them back together. It will take you to the Cyberverse police station. From there you should be able to locate their physical bodies with a recall routine."

"Good luck," you say, as Nelson activates his transport-link. It is hard to tell in the chaos, but you think you recognize Greg lying beside Heran. You hope they are all right.

You run toward the four figures. Most of the bat creatures are concentrating on the police still fighting in the air, but you still have a number of close calls in the short distance that you travel. You open the cage door and, with a quick flip, cover the unconscious figures with the net. Then you activate the emergency prisoner recall function. In an instant, you and the prisoners are gone from the battlefield.

Suddenly, you find yourself in a jail cell of the Cyberverse police station. You shout for help. Guards come and release you and take the former hostages to the virtual infirmary, where a team of computer doctors and nurses will immediately begin working on the strangely still virtual bodies.

"Are they going to be okay?" you ask one of the doctors rushing past.

Turn to page 22.

"Let's try the swamp," you tell Heran.

"Come on, then," she replies. "We have to get to the access portal. The gorillas will be here any minute."

With these words Heran takes off into the forest of floating trees. Cruising through branches, roots, and thick trunks, you quickly become disoriented, but Heran seems to know where she's going. After a few minutes, she stops in front of a marble platform. "Here we are. Now comes the fun part."

"What do we do?" you ask.

"First, we both have to get up on the platform," she says. She steps up onto it. You notice rows of intricate lines swirling over its flat surface. The lines are almost invisible from a direct angle, but as you turn your eyes, patterns and shapes appear and fade. "Then we activate it by asking it to take us to the swamp. Get up, or we'll be dropped into different places."

You climb up onto the platform. An electric thrill races through your body. You wonder if this platform might lead to other places besides the swamp.

"Ready?" Heran asks.

You nod. She continues, directing the platform this time, "Okay. Take us to the swamp!"

One moment you are in the middle of the forest, and the next you are up to your knees in thick, black mud. Shrill animal cries rise around you from all sides.

Turn to page 8.

"Let's swing the cages and smash them together," you tell Heran. "If it works, we can get out of here before the frog-beings come back."

Heran nods. "Okay, on the count of three," you say. "One, two . . . three!"

At first the cages barely move, but once you get them started, they pick up momentum and really begin to swing. Before long, the two are hitting each other. "Hang on," you yell. After a few nondamaging brushes, the contact increases, and you hear a satisfying *crunch*!

One corner of your cage has crumpled. The creatures writhing in the water below you erupt into a high state of frenzy. *Wham!* Another blow, and a hole appears in your cage. If you time it right, you can slip out on the back swing and land on firm ground.

"I'm going to jump," you shout as the cages come together once more. Heran nods grimly. The bottom of her prison popped off on the last impact, and only her hands clenched around the bars are keeping her inside. You let go and land in the water, but near the edge.

Turn to page 57.

52

In one burst of movement, you spring up, grab the tag and some tools, and jump headfirst out of the hole. Suddenly, you see that you are about to crash into a tree. The impact scatters the things you grabbed. As you watch them drift away your hopes fade. Your shoulder hurts, and the pain is very real.

You start to climb down from the tree you landed in. At the bottom you see a white gorilla holding your tag. How in the Cyberverse are you going to get it back?

You feel ready to give up. Throwing caution to the wind, you storm toward the gorilla, grab the tag, and take off. The pool through which you entered this nightmare is right there, and the gorilla is standing motionless, stunned by your actions. You're going to make it!

With a splash, you flop into the water. It's hard to tell, but you think the tag is working. As you break the pool's surface, you tap in a code on the directory of the tag. If it works, the tag should send an emergency signal to Greg and hopefully to the police. Now you just have to avoid the enraged gorilla at the water's edge.

"Don't come in," you shout to the gorilla. "The water's cold, and the fish will bite your toes."

The gorilla hovers next to the pool, unwilling to come in after you. After a while ten more gorillas show up. You stay in the middle of the pool, treading water.

Turn to page 76.

As soon as you are back in the physical world, you call the police and tell them what you saw. After some initial disbelief, they agree to check things out.

You return home and soon receive a call from the police. They tell you they found Shenda in room thirty-seven, just as you thought. They found her physical body checked into a hospital as an unknown person. She was tired and confused, but she'll be all right.

"You shouldn't have done what you did," the officer goes on to tell you. "You could have ended up in the same state as Shenda—or worse. Nonetheless, we have to thank you for your help."

"Don't worry," you tell the officer. "I'm not about to do a repeat performance. Right now the last thing that I want to see is the inside of a computer."

The End

54

BEEP. Time to awaken for school. BEEP. Time to awaken for school.

For once, you are actually happy to hear your alarm go off in the morning. All night long, you had nightmares about a swarm of insects trying to smother you. No matter how fast you ran, they caught up with you and trapped you.

During the magnatrain ride to school you attempt to do your homework, but your mind keeps going back to the message you received last night.

You don't have a class with Greg until after lunch, so you decide to leave him a message. Whoever sent you last night's e-mail might be able to track your computer activities, so you write out a note and put it in Greg's desk. Sometimes simplicity is best—besides, you don't know what else to do.

At 12:15, you are in the Food Wheel on level 3. You sit quietly, eating the processed bean curd roll that has drained almost all your credits. As you eat, you look around and wonder if anyone is watching you.

"Mind if I sit here?"

You look up in surprise and see a girl from your school. You don't know her name, but you've seen her in the halls. "I'm kind of waiting for someone," you tell her.

"Actually, I'm the one you're waiting for. Sorry I'm late."

Turn to page 39.

Carefully watching the beast and the old man, you continue to talk. "Doesn't seem like you get much company here in your living quarters," you say.

"These aren't my living quarters," the old man replies, turning his attention to the beast. Moving cautiously, he places one shriveled hand on the creature's head between the sharp protrusions of horn. "Gorgo and I just come here to work. Our space is beyond. Once I gave up the real world, I refused to be limited by its restrictions. That's why I built this place."

"Oh," you murmur. Nonchalantly you stretch, get to your feet, and take a step toward the worktable. "How long have you been here? It looks like you've spent a lot of time and effort creating this game."

"I did, but for more than simple self-amusement," the old man says, staring directly at you. "I designed this place to deal with those who felt they must pry, like you. When you tried to steal my secrets, my work, you signed your own sentence. Thieves deserve no mercy."

This is not where you wanted the conversation to go. The old man is getting so excited that his face twitches and jumps. Gorgo gets up and begins to growl.

"What's your name?" you blurt out, unable to think of anything else to say.

Turn to page 31.

56

"Well, there's no time like the present," you tell yourself, as you get out of bed and dress in the dark. This time you won't drag Greg with you into the mess.

You sneak quietly out of your house into the main corridors. Once outside, in the fast-paced pulse of the city's corridors, you realize just how exhausted you are. But you feel you have to do something to help find Shenda.

After a few level changes, you are at the rows of public access computer terminals. Unlike the one that you and Greg used the other day, these terminals allow full access into the Cyberverse, and their cost reflects that. Putting in all the credits you have saved up for the last six months only gives you an hour and a half of time. The way these expensive terminals stay in business is by offering the luxury of anonymity. If you pay in hard credits, there is no way anyone can trace your excursion. But now you have only an hour and a half to find Shenda.

The desert motif is still in effect when you immerse yourself into the Cyberverse. A few sites, you notice, have switched to jungle scenes. You head for the brown building. It's still there and still looks just like a plain brown box. You don't get too close this time. Your guess is that Shenda came here to look around for clues.

Turn to page 35.

Moving as quickly as you can, you scramble up onto the mud plain. A tentacle slaps at your leg, but you keep going. You turn to see how Heran is doing. She is sprawled in the mud on the other side of the water.

You splash through the narrowest part of the inlet that separates you from Heran, just barely avoiding the water monsters. Rushing to her, you drag her toward the platform.

Heran crawls up beside you onto the dais and collects herself for a moment. Then she calmly speaks. "Command-Q, exit procedure, force quit!" she says. Suddenly you are out of the swamp.

Turn to page 41.

58

You've been through too much to let that twisted creature escape. You take the plasma rifle and tracer-link from Officer Nelson's hands.

"What are you doing? Wait!" he yells, as you activate the tracer-link. But he's too late. Positioning the unfamiliar plasma rifle in your grip, you prepare yourself for the unknown.

With a loud *pop,* you appear in a world of liquid shapes and colors. Undulating spheres of jellylike substance float around you. Your view is obscured by the ever-moving shapes. You feel completely disoriented.

"Where are you?" you yell into the pulsating background. You receive no reply. As you float there amidst the moving shapes, you try and figure out what to do next. There is no obvious place in which to find a little old madman, and you begin to have a sneaking suspicion.

"He wanted me to follow him," you mutter. "Just like he wanted us to find the link to the place where he had all those creatures at his disposal. This is all some sort of elaborate trap. I bet he let me escape simply to make his game more interesting."

As all the pieces start to make sense, you decide to find a way to beat the old man at his own game. You hit the recall button on your police body, but nothing happens. Deep down, you already knew he would have taken care of such details.

From behind you, you hear a cackle. "Not only did I get you again, my amusing little friend," the old man says, "I also got a score of police officers to test my new creations on." The next thing you know, you have been absorbed into one of the floating blobs. You can't move.

Turn to page 34.

60

"Okay, Heran," you say. "Let's give that prize a shot."

"Keep your fingers crossed," she replies. "This could just make things worse." She removes a small round black object from her pocket. Spines of various sizes protrude from it. Pausing for a moment, she sets the prize down on the floor of her cage, then pushes something on its surface.

Immediately your situation changes. In an instant the prize expands to twice the height of the cages. As it does, the wicker explodes into fragments. The black object blows up like a giant, spiky bubble.

"It's a shield bubble!" Heran shouts. "It'll protect us if we're inside it. Hurry!" Quickly you jump through the spikes into the prize's interior. Below your feet you can see one of the swamp monsters attacking the surface of the sphere. Luckily you are floating on the water instead of sinking into the mess of monsters and mud.

The sphere moves with you, like an ordinary ball, when you walk. You and Heran head away from the ruined cages and the swamp.

Turn to page 43.

62

Before you know it, you are in the access level. Fanning out in a pattern, the officers check all connections that could possibly be linked to unknown mainframes. You try to keep out of their way.

"Lieutenant," a voice says over the priority channel, "we found pay dirt. Whoever made this place wasn't figuring on getting caught. These links are so obvious a child could find them."

"That's what worries me," O'Reilly replies. "But we don't have much choice. Set up the override transmitter and go after the guy."

Setting up the transmitter takes only a few minutes. The team members get ready for another shift in locale. Moving in twos, they are transmitted to the unknown mainframe. After a bit of waiting, it is your turn.

In a flash, you are in midair, but this time your virtual body can fly. "It's a trap!" someone shouts over the communications channel. The sky is thick with flying bodies, smoke, and fire. Officer Nelson grabs you by the arm and heads down to the ground.

→

"Watch my back," he tells you as you both land. He calmly fires his plasma rifle at an oncoming virtual monster—a giant, batlike creature. He destroys it, but three more take its place. The mass of virtual creatures seems endless. You watch as two officers materialize in the air, only to be immediately attacked. One starts to fall slowly to the ground.

You notice between attacks that the creatures are taking off from a black hill in the distance.

"Over there," you say, pointing. "That's where he is."

"How do you know?" Nelson screams as he shoots two bat-monsters.

"I just do." You begin running toward the hill.

Turn to page 78.

64

You decide to say yes to Shenda. You do not want to end up in jail—real *or* virtual. Plus, joining her may give you a cool opportunity to learn about another side of the Cyberverse. But you'd better go find Greg and tell him what you're getting him into.

You catch up to him as the class start alert rings at the end of lunch. "What's up?" he asks.

The cafeteria is full of rushing students. Suddenly you don't feel safe talking to him here. "I can't talk about it right now. You free after school?"

Greg looks at you quizzically. "Yeah, sure. Come over to my place."

The rest of the day crawls by. As soon as school lets out, you and Greg head for the magnatrain's main access tubes. Soon you are in the safety of his room. The clutter of computer equipment, sports gear, and clothes strewn about the floor reassures your disturbed sense of normalcy.

You immediately tell him about Shenda. "The police are on to us. They want us to work with them on some case. But I'm not sure if this Shenda person is who she says she is."

"Only one way to find out, don't you think?" Greg says. "We've got to go back into the 'verse and check her out at the Well. We're already in this far. What more can they do to us?"

Turn to page 94.

With that, Shenda enters the room and sets down a tray of drinks and cookies. The look in her virtual eyes betrays nothing, and you are not sure if she is even aware you are there.

"Do not worry," Mestopheles says. "You will be joining her soon enough, and then there will be no worries."

The End

66

Eventually a figure materializes before you. A bright light burns out from its body; it hurts to look at it. You wonder if this is some strange form of torture.

"You are not authorized to enter," the figure finally says. "Are you from the Nagasaki Corporation?"

"I'm just a kid, and I'm lost," you say. "Please let me go. I haven't done anything."

"That does not matter. You have entered the BMB Computer Facility without permission. The punishment is service. You will be integrated into our computer system. Your mind will become a processor of information. Your consciousness will be removed from any attachment to the physical world. Like a single neuron in a brain, your role is now that of a part."

"I'll do whatever you want. Just let me go," you plead.

"Yes, you will do what we want. But you will never go," the figure says, coming toward you. It's the last thing you remember before you lose consciousness.

When you wake again, your place in the order of things is well-defined. There is no pain, no pleasure, only tasks. You have no emotions—they are not necessary to the operation of a computer. But you are still aware. You still have memories, and your past life is fully accessible. If you had any emotion left, you would hate the role that you now fill. Work is all you have. You are part of a unit, no longer an individual.

The End

Two weeks pass. You are doing a casual review of your electronic files when you notice something extra in them. There is a memory discrepancy between what is visible on the desktop of your computer and what is actually there.

"What's going on?" you mutter. You decide to do a check from the Cyberverse. Even though none of your special tags has signaled an alarm, you have the feeling that this is not some simple data malfunction.

Like many people who use the Cyberverse regularly, you've programmed a semipermanent "building" for yourself that acts as a physical manifestation of your computer's presence in the Cyberverse. The style that you chose is a re-creation of a ruined Mayan temple.

You enter the temple—the virtual site of your computer—and move directly to the storage area with the strange memory discrepancy. You log in your personal code to enter the room that houses your memory. Once inside, you feel a strong sense of disorientation.

Suddenly you are floating in a deep pool of water, with giant trees growing in and around the pool. Roots dangle down from above, and branches with lush leaves spring directly from the earth. Some trees are upside down. There are pine, spruce, mahogany, willow, cypress, olive, and redwood trees, all growing next to each other.

"Got you!" a voice booms from above.

Turn to page 97.

After a few minutes, you reach your destination in the industrial sector, a building that looks like a small brown box. Set against the Cyberverse background of wild colors and randomly moving scenes, this brown box grabs your attention. Anyplace that goes so far out of its way to avoid standing out must have something interesting inside it.

Navigating in the Cyberverse is difficult and sometimes dangerous, but it's nothing compared to breaking into a well-defended information system. Luckily you've brought along your special code-cracking program. The program simulates an attack on your target, and while the target's attention is distracted, the code-cracking program inserts a wedge into it. The wedge allows only a tiny amount of data to be transferred to you, but sometimes this tiny amount is all you need.

You set the wedge carefully and prepare yourself for the influx of new information. Signaling to Greg, you get ready to start the process. You touch a large button on the side of the wedge program, launching it toward the featureless building. But before the target is hit, you and Greg are engulfed in a sticky mass of red foam.

Greg's virtual body writhes in the grip of the foam, and you struggle to reach your disconnect module. Each time you come close to the safety recall, you are overcome with more restraints. The vivid colors of the Cyberverse fade to pitch-black.

Turn to page 26.

As you watch, the virtual world goes crazy. The hole in the sky freezes, as do the creatures that were streaming out of it. The top of the tower is suddenly gone. The green player explodes into light, leaving the limp body of a normal virtual human.

A new voice booms from above. "System Error. System Error. Automatic shutdown." The next thing you are conscious of, you are back in your room, in your physical body, with your helmet on. Your trip back to the physical world must have been more violent than usual. You lie twitching on your bed for a while. When you are able to, you call the police to tell them what happened. They tell you that they have already begun an investigation into this weird game, but they have no leads.

The End

This time you don't see the familiar landmarks of the 'verse. The special immersion unit you're using is too powerful—everything appears instead as great fluxing waves of energy. One wave comes directly at you. You barely have time to activate the navigation commands to avoid it.

"Find the brown building," Officer Ramirez says over your direct line.

It takes you a while to get there. You have trouble locating the building, and you soon see why. The brown building has become a black box.

"There it is," you tell the officer. "They must have . . ." You trail off as you notice that the building absorbs anything that goes near it.

"It's a trap!" you cry out. But you're too late. As Ramirez begins his dive into the building, you feel yourself being cut off from your physical body.

The End

You decide to make a break for it. There's no time to warn Greg. Once he sees what you are doing, he'll figure out your plan soon enough. The police are moving toward you now—you have to act or miss your chance.

"Don't worry, officers, I'll be right along," you say, as you depress the emergency recall button.

Green light surrounds you. You have the sensation of being pulled apart and then squished back together again. Leaving the Cyberverse is always disorienting. This time the strangeness of the feeling is reassuring; it means the recall is working. The light fades and darkness takes its place. In a flash you see Greg's room. His physical body is propped against his bed, but before you can reach over to hit his recall button, the darkness comes back and you feel as if you are being scattered once again.

Turn to page 82.

You decide it's best to just let the police handle the search for Shenda. Still, throughout the next day at school, you worry that you have made the wrong choice. You wish you could help somehow.

"Please pay attention during class time," Mrs. Hargrove tells you.

There is no time, or reason, to explain why you are distracted. You just reply, "Yes, Mrs. Hargrove. I'm sorry."

"Precisely my thought. You are very sorry looking." The class laughs at her joke. "I was going over last night's material. Please try to pay attention, even if you are not going to participate."

You just let her comments go. Normally her teasing would make you angry, but all you can think about is Shenda.

As soon as the bell signals, you scramble to leave as quickly as possible, but you see Mrs. Hargrove coming toward you. This time the playful expression is gone from her face. You wonder if she is going to lecture you some more about your behavior.

"Please wait a moment," she says. "I've just received a message from the principal. He wants you to go directly to his office. Apparently a police officer wants to see you." Mrs. Hargrove pauses and looks at you closely. "Are you in some sort of trouble? Is that why you were so distracted today?"

Turn to page 96.

74

You decide to tell Shenda that you can't help her. You don't really want to work for the police. You admire their fight against real criminals, but you don't agree with arresting people who use the Cyberverse for free speech and political purposes. Besides, you don't know for sure whether Shenda really *is* working for the police.

"Well, what is your decision?" Shenda asks when you meet her the next day.

"I gave your offer a lot of thought," you begin, "but I don't feel comfortable about working with the police."

"That's what I thought," she replies. "Unfortunately, if you do not choose to work with us, we'll have to bring you up on charges of attempted breaking and entering a private data bank."

"What? I thought you said you had more important people to arrest."

"That might be true if you were to work for us. But if you continue to ignore our laws, we have no choice."

You're angry. "If you think you can blackmail me into working for you, you're out of your mind!"

"Please come with me," Shenda replies. "I have to take you down to the station to be booked."

"No way—" you begin. Then you notice the plasma pistol Shenda has pointed at you. "Okay. But you can put the gun away," you tell her. Instead of replying, Shenda motions you to the exit with her pistol.

Turn to page 24.

You can't just leave Greg here. It's probably a better idea to come clean with the police now.

"Look, officers, I have no idea about any abduction, but I'll come with you to help you figure out what's going on." You hear Greg breathe a sigh of relief.

"Come with us down to the station. We'll notify your parents in the physical world." With that you are taken into the large transport program and quickly shuttled to the Cyberverse virtual police station. The transport's programming allows you to fly through the security perimeters around the police station. Everything in this jail is clean and perfect, but you know deep down in your virtual bones that it is a real jail.

"All right, we know certain facts about your activities during the last few days, and things don't look good for you." The voice comes from a large blue figure who visits you and Greg in your holding cell after you've been waiting there an hour and a half. "Your attempted infiltration of a private data bank was small-time but still illegal. We might have let that slide, but the other matter—that is too serious."

"What are you talking about?" you blurt. "I admit that we were trying to get into that data bank, but we haven't done anything else. I swear."

Turn to page 100.

Just as you are considering making a break for it through the gang of gorillas, a squad of police materializes. Some flicker in and out of existence as they tune their immersion packs. One fires a tube with a big flaring nozzle. A writhing net of energy clasps one gorilla after another and makes them disappear.

"Are you the citizen who used the illegal signaling device?" a police officer asks you.

"Yes. I'm so glad you showed up. This whole place is a twisted death-game," you say, as you swim to the edge of the pool. "I've been running around trying to keep from being killed."

"Save it for the detectives, kid. Our job is rescue, not investigation. Let's get you back to the station," the officer says, as she helps you to your feet.

"May I just go back to the physical world, and then go to the station? I'm sick of this virtual universe."

"Permission granted. We'll send someone by your house," the officer says, attaching an emergency recall program to your body. "Rest if you can."

Your reintegration is painful and lengthy. You lie still in your physical body for a long time before moving. Crawling into bed, you try to sleep as you wait for the police.

→

Later, down at the station, you find out that as soon as you were rescued, a self-destruct erase command was triggered on the game. Some clues were recovered, but no one saw an old man with a demon. Apparently the programming was much more complicated than anything available to the general public, or even the government.

Turn to page 20.

The police are doing a good job of destroying the bat-monsters. Already there seem to be fewer of them. But hordes of white gorillas surround the hill. Flashes of lightning illuminate the scene from time to time. During one of these flashes you see four figures caught in a large cage on the hilltop.

"Come on!" you shout to the other officers as you continue running toward the hill. Now you can see that one of the four figures inside the cage is Heran. None of them is moving.

As two beasts that could be Gorgo's twins lead a pack of screaming gorillas toward you, you catch a glimpse of a gnarled figure hopping up and down near the cage. "He's here," you yell. "Over on this hill!"

"Move in an alpha pattern to the objective," the lieutenant says over the com-link. You watch as the officers organize themselves into a wedge and start approaching the hill. New groups of gorillas and bat-monsters begin a fresh attack, but the officers calmly dispose of them as quickly as they appear.

"I know you!" the old man shrieks as you get closer to the top of the black hill. "Your police body cannot hide you from me!"

Turn to page 80.

80

"Give yourself up," you say, trying to sound author-itative. The police are busy with the virtual monsters, and you are on your own for the moment. "You can't get away."

"Can't I? Watch this!" His wrinkled face contorts into a horrible grimace. Then he simply vanishes. The gorillas and bat creatures continue to attack as if nothing has happened.

"Can we set up a tracer-link that will track where he went?" you yell into your com-unit.

Turn to page 19.

Five desperate leaps and six trees later, you reach the top of a maple and find that you have nowhere else to go. To the right, you see a shimmering red spot. You move to get a better view, thinking about what to do. The spot ripples. Every now and then, you glimpse something beyond its edges.

Maybe the spot is a transporter to another area. Or maybe it's a trap. Your only other option is climbing back down the tree. But that means taking your chances with the gorillas. Of course, each second that you wait, the apes get closer.

If you want to risk leaping into the red spot, turn to page 42.

If you decide to climb down the tree, turn to page 38.

82

When you come to, you don't know where you are. Looking around, all you see are featureless walls. A gray light pulses and glows.

"Look, I'm sorry I tried to run away," you yell. "I was scared. I didn't want to go to jail."

"You are not precisely in jail," a voice replies from above. "Rather, you are, in fact, my prisoner."

"Who are you?"

"I am an information merchant. My business is providing service and security to discerning individuals and corporations. You, my young friend, have jeopardized my business." The voice pauses. "I need people who can help me with my projects. People who can discover and learn, and then relay that information back to me. Information is power both here and in the physical world. It would be awkward for others to discover that the Planetary Government is contracting with me to gather certain infoblocks essential to their plans."

Turn to page 86.

"Well, the gorillas were great, but I liked the weird trees the best," you say, keeping your body still but searching everywhere you can with your vision.

"Thank you. Simply take a normal scene and alter one key component, like the placement of the trees, and you have something strange enough to disturb," he says. "No one really appreciates what I do."

You pretend to focus all your attention on the beast, but you're really examining the equipment-covered table. On it is one of the alert tags you made for your computer. "Oh, *I* appreciate what you do," you say, hoping to distract the old man. If the tag is activated, an alarm will beep Greg and let him know that something bad has happened to you.

You look a little closer and see that your tag has been taken apart. Will it still work? You can't tell without getting up, and you don't want to attract any more attention than you have to.

"I was amazed at the level of realism here," you continue. "Even when I was climbing for my life." Should you grab the tag and make a break for it back through the red hole and into the game? Jumping out of a hole in the sky does not sound fun, but neither does trying to fix a software program while an insane old man and his pet demon try to kill you.

Turn to page 25.

A few moments after entering the area, you see the tracking probes. You watch as they attach themselves to your duplicate body and lift it away. While this is happening, you have time to look around. You spot a small access hatch. It might let you enter the brown building's data bank without being discovered.

Until now your plan was simply to follow whatever took your duplicates, hoping it would lead you to Shenda. This hatch might offer a faster way to retrieve information. Should you follow the probes, or go in through the access hatch—and find your way on your own?

If you decide to follow the probes,
turn to page 90.

If you choose to enter the access hatch,
turn to page 16.

You help the girl to her feet. "Sorry. I didn't mean to throw you like that, but you surprised me. Where can we go from here, anyway? I climbed as high as I could, but all I saw was a red spot floating in the air."

"My name is Heran. I've been here for at least a year, maybe longer," she says in a rush. "No one knows why we're here. You're lucky you did not go for the red spot. I doubt you are ready for that yet. I have to figure out if I'm going to go to the challenge rounds or not. Do you want to come?"

"I'm not sure," you reply. "What are my options?"

"I came here to the pool because this is one of the main access points for the game," Heran replies. "But I don't know if I want to try getting to the end through the swamp or through the challenge rounds."

"The what?"

"The challenge rounds are a series of battles that you can enter to win placement or bonuses," Heran tells you. "You have to fight an exact replica of a body that is randomly generated for you. You are both completely equal, except for your mind. If you win, you get a prize. If you lose, prizes don't really matter anymore. Most people try the swamp, but no one has ever come back to tell whether it leads to the real world or not."

Turn to page 27.

You're not sure just what you've done to upset this person, but you apologize anyway. "I'm sorry. I truly am," you say.

"Luckily for you, you did not succeed in your endeavor." The voice lowers its tone, and you have to strain to hear each word. "I have decided to give you a chance. Your skills and talents are quite good, for an amateur."

"Who are you? What's going on here?"

"Who I am is a long story. You are faced with a choice right now. Unfortunately this choice has only one correct answer. Work with me. Work hard and I will reward you well. Turn me down, and you become a body without a soul. A sad little puppet with its strings cut."

"That's not much of a choice, but I'll go along with you," you say, thinking that the first chance you get, you will go to the police.

"There is no turning back. Do not think of crossing me. I have your life-pattern hardwired to many different monitors. Your life is information, and as I said, my business is information." As the voice finishes, the walls of your cell dissolve, and you find yourself sitting on a plush couch. Mahogany, leather, and books surround you. Directly across from where you are sitting stands a man. His back is to you.

→

"Let me continue now that you are a bit more comfortable," the man says without turning. "Much is at my disposal, but my greatest possession is power. I will share some of that power, but it must be earned."

"Okay," you say. "But I still don't know your name."

"Call me Mephistopheles."

Turn to page 65.

"So, aren't you going to arrest me?" you finally ask her. "You just said that you saw the whole thing."

"Well, you guys are really just kids. Arresting you would be pointless, since you didn't actually break into the building." She pauses. "I wanted to see if you would be willing to help us in our investigation."

"What investigation?" you ask, trying not to bristle at the "just kids" comment.

"I can't tell you that unless you agree to work with us."

"What if I say no?"

"I can't make you any promises if you say no," she replies.

"I see. You'll have to let me think about this for a little while," you say. You try to keep calm. Can you trust Shenda?

"All right, let me know by this time tomorrow. I have to run some cyberrands anyway. Bye." You watch Shenda walk away.

If you decide to join Shenda and the Cyberverse Police Force in their investigation, turn to page 64.

If you tell her Thanks but no thanks, turn to page 74.

You head out of the room. The darkness of the rest area is obliterated by a blaze of light. There is no sun. The directionless light of the 'verse makes everything appear flat. To your right you see a large tower that juts into the air. Then you notice the spectators.

Row upon row of virtual bodies pack the stands forty levels deep. Many are standing and waving their hands. As a loud roar builds from the crowd, you see what they are cheering for—two huge virtual creatures are battling with blows of lightning and fire. They have faces like monsters, and each has three pairs of arms.

"Those are two players," Heran says from your side. "You can tell by the color coding on the battle armor. Looks like an exciting match, but the one in the red is going to lose."

Almost immediately after Heran speaks, the fighter with the green armor slips a close-range lightning blast past the red fighter's shield. With a flash and a ripple, all the red player's arms fly off, and a smaller body slips out of the big red shell. It hits the sand and lies still. The crowd starts leaping and shouting. A few spectators jump out of the stands and rush toward the green player.

A crackle of blue electricity swirls around the tower, and the same voice that you heard by the pool comes down from the sky.

Turn to page 18.

There's no time to sit and daydream—you have to follow those probes before you lose them. They lift off with the duplicate of your virtual body into the artificial sky of the Cyberverse. You follow them by skating across the gleaming sand of the desert environment. Skating is not nearly as fast as flying, but you know that using your flying program here would make you too visible.

You follow the probes around to the opposite side of the building. Turning the corner, you see where they are headed, and you feel your virtual stomach tighten. The probes are aimed at a high-speed computer-to-computer network. Directly linked computers can transfer data extremely rapidly, which is generally a good thing. But you have no idea where in the Cyberverse the transfer computer is located. The electronic note that you sent the police only mentioned that you were going to the brown building. If you follow the transfer, the police won't be able to find you should anything happen.

Turn to page 102.

During the days that follow, you keep moving. Occasionally bands of frog-beings find you in the sphere and attack. They give up when they realize they cannot get at you. Heran thinks that leaving the sphere will cause it to deactivate permanently, and since, in your virtual bodies, you do not need to eat or drink, you stay inside. This tiny sphere in a swamp may be where you spend eternity.

The End

Nice work. For a bunch of small-timers, you did a pretty good job of infiltrating, but you'll need help now that they know about you. Meet me in the Food Wheel on level 3 tomorrow at noon.

—A Friend

P.S.—In the future, don't use your personal debit card to pay for an illegitimate immersion.

You're surprised by this message—and more than a little nervous. Who did it come from, and how does the sender know about you? Should you trust and go to meet him or her? Or should you ignore the message completely? You have to make a decision before tomorrow morning.

If you decide to meet the mysterious message sender, turn to page 54.

If you decide not to meet the person who sent the message, turn to page 99.

You shake your head, but you know he's right. Going to the Well is not illegal, but it's still something you'd rather not do.

The Well may be used by anyone who has access to the Cyberverse. There's only one catch—each time you go to it for information, you have to give it some new information of your own in exchange. It sounds easy, but since everyone uses the Well, only the most personal and delicate secrets remain new information. Once that information is absorbed, it is available to anyone who uses the interface.

"Here's an extra input helmet if you don't have yours," Greg says. He is all ready to go. "Let's get this over with before my parents come home."

"Okay," you reply. You put the helmet on and key in your personal immersion code. Greg's home mainframe has plenty of power for a full immersion, so you don't need the booster. But everything you do will be carefully recorded and stored.

The Cyberverse orientation sequence follows the familiar pattern of disorientation and déjà vu. In the distance, you feel the gentle slipping of control from your physical body to the computer simulation. With a sharp mental snap, you are suddenly fully in the Cyberverse.

→

Each day or so, the Cyberverse's virtual background is changed. Today the theme is desert. Bright beams of light crisscross broad expanses of amber and gold. The commercial buildings have all been reimaged to look like pyramids. The entertainment centers have Egyptian-style ornamentation. Tearing yourself away from the sights surrounding you, you see Greg motioning you to get going.

With a free software transportation program that is automatically downloaded when you enter the Cyberverse, your virtual bodies set out like skaters across a frozen lake of sand.

Turn to page 46.

"Maybe," you say. "I'd better go."

By the time you arrive at the principal's office, you have a black hole of worry in your stomach. The officer is waiting there for you.

"I'm Officer Ramirez," he says. "I interviewed you the other day."

"I remember, but it was more of an interrogation than an interview."

"True, but now we need your help. Principal Donner has told me you have been helping the school with some of its computer problems. We need those skills to find Shenda. Will you help?"

"Of course," you answer without hesitation. "I'll do whatever I can."

"Good. I've brought a special immersion unit for you. With this unit, I have access to most of the secure areas in the Cyberverse, but I need an experienced navigator to help me stay on track."

"Let's do it," you say bravely.

Instead of the usual individual helmets, Officer Ramirez brings out a double unit with lots of interconnecting wires. Placing one helmet on your head and the other on his own, he plugs the whole unit into the principal's terminal. With the flick of a switch you are suddenly in the Cyberverse.

Turn to page 71.

You scramble out of the pool, wondering what's going on. This is definitely not part of the temple you designed. So much for your code; whoever trapped you here is clearly a master of programming. The thought does not cheer you up, nor does the return of the voice.

"You are now in the game, my friend. Survive and you might become useful. Die here, and you die in the physical world as well. Get to the end, solve the puzzle, and we'll have a nice chat."

"Who are you? What do you want with me?" you shout. But you have no time to listen for a reply. White gorillas are moving through the trees directly at you. They do not look friendly.

You search frantically for a way out. All you can see is forest and the pool that you just climbed out of. Not knowing what else to do, you grab a tree branch and start to climb.

At the top of the tree, you realize you will need to jump to a large spruce close by to continue your ascent. With a strong push, you sail into the space between you and the prickly branches. Your landing is difficult, but you hang on. Looking down, you see the gorillas coming quickly after you. You go back to climbing.

Turn to page 81.

"All right, let's try the challenge rounds," you tell Heran. "At least we'll know something about what we are getting into."

"Come on, the entrance is along the edge of the pool." Heran runs ahead of you toward the water's edge. Without hesitating, she dives in. Her head pops up from the surface. "Down here," she says, before diving under again.

As you rush over, you hear the grunts of gorillas above you. Diving in, you search for Heran and the entrance to the challenge rounds. Beneath a shelf of rock, you see a pulsing area of blue and yellow that Heran is swimming into. You follow. As soon as your hand touches the surface, you are transported.

Wet, and lying flat on your stomach, you find yourself in a dark room with sand for a floor and wooden slats for walls. Through the spaces between the slats you see other figures moving around outside the room.

"I'm glad you made it," Heran says as you sit up.

"Who's out there?" you ask.

"Those are spectators and the other players."

"How do we play?" you ask.

"Just go to the center of the arena and ask for a match. This place is our rest area. If you think you are going to lose, you can try to make it back here. If you do make it back, you simply forfeit the match. If you don't, your opponent will probably kill you."

Turn to page 89.

You decide not to meet the person who sent you the message. The next day at school you spend a lot of time watching the other students and teachers, wondering if any of them sent it. By the time Greg meets you after school, you are exhausted from being constantly on guard. You tell him about the message.

"I didn't show for the meeting," you tell him. "What do you think?"

"I'm not sure," Greg responds. "If it is someone who wants to help us, doing nothing won't matter. And answering an anonymous message might put you in a bad situation. It's like an admission that you did something wrong."

"I guess I'll just act as though nothing has happened," you say. "But I still feel nervous."

Over the next few days you start to relax, but you also take precautions. Using all the programming skills you have, you construct new security devices to cover your personal files. There isn't much in them, but you feel better knowing you are protected. Instead of simple barriers, you devise a series of tags that will allow partial entry into your system. If someone does try to enter your personal files, the tags will automatically move the intruder into a sanitized version of your stuff that does not contain anything really interesting. At the same time, an internal alarm will signal you that an intrusion is occurring.

Turn to page 67.

"The last contact we had from Shenda Lang was a message explaining that she was going to meet you for lunch. No one has seen her since. Then we get a notification that someone is fishing for information about her in the Well. I believe you have a lot of explaining to do."

"Trust me," you tell the officer. "The only reason I was checking up on Shenda was that she asked me to help out the Cyberverse Police Force. I wanted to make sure she was who she said she was." You pause. "Besides, I was back in class a few minutes after leaving the Food Wheel. Shenda met me at 12:15, we talked until 12:35, and I was in my history class at 12:40. How could I have done anything?"

"We'll check on that, but right now I want you to tell me all about your little excursion into the Cyberverse the other day. Don't leave anything out."

After an hour of intensive questioning, you have told your story three times over. You are interrupted by a private call to the officer.

When he returns, he grudgingly tells you, "It looks like you were telling the truth earlier. We've received confirmation from your school about your whereabouts."

You don't try to hide your relief. "Great! When can I go home?"

→

"You seem like a good kid, and I'm glad you did not have anything to do with Shenda's abduction." The officer sighs deeply. "Unfortunately, now we have no leads. She just disappeared—but no one just disappears in the physical world."

"I'm sorry," you say.

Another officer comes to the cell and leads you out to the virtual jail's lobby, where Greg is waiting for you.

"Howdy," he says. "Let's get out of here!"

"I couldn't agree more," you reply. You both hit your recall buttons.

Turn to page 10.

The thought troubles you for only a moment. You don't even pause in your skating, following the probes directly toward the terminal that will transport you to an unknown computer.

Once you are inside the network and being transferred to the end site, you have no room for thought. The compression programs do not allow for complete consciousness, so the trip seems instantaneous to you.

Once you are through, you stand still for a few moments, trying to get your bearings. All around you are corridors. Each one is color coded, with rows of evenly spaced doors as far as you can see. In the distance, you see the probes turning the corner of one of the corridors.

Turn to page 28.

Later, you find out that the tracking squad traced the old man back to a mainframe housed in a pyramid in the physical world. Rather than be captured, he allowed his consciousness to dissipate into the chaos of the Cyberverse. He is now a small part of everything in the Cyberverse, and that thought makes you cringe. You still don't understand the reasons behind what happened, but you are glad that the whole thing is—you hope—over.

The End

ABOUT THE AUTHOR

ANSON MONTGOMERY is a graduate of Williams College with a degree in ancient history. He is a developer of interactive multimedia projects for both children and adults. Anson enjoys skiing, mountain biking, chess, comic books, and fiction. He has written three other books for the Choose Your Own Adventure Series.

ABOUT THE ILLUSTRATOR

ERIC CHERRY's first artistic influence was his father, a Washington, D.C., police artist who taught him the basics of illustration while finishing his sketches at the dining room table. Eric lives in New York City, where he studies under Frank Mason at the Art Students League.